Chickens

by Bobby Lynn Maslen
pictures by John R. Maslen

Scholastic Inc.
New York • Toronto • London • Auckland • Sydney • Mexico City • New Delhi • Hong Kong • Buenos Aires

Available Bob Books®:

Set 1: Beginning Readers — With consistent new sounds added gradually, your new reader is gently introduced to all the letters of the alphabet. They can soon say, "I read the whole book!®"

Set 2: Advancing Beginners — The use of three-letter words and consistent vowel sounds in slightly longer stories build skill and confidence.

Set 3: Word Families — Consonant blends, endings and a few sight words advance reading skills while the use of word families keep reading manageable.

Set 4: Complex Words — Longer books and complex words engage young readers as proficiency advances.

Set 5: Long Vowels — Silent *e* and other vowel blends build young readers' vocabulary and aptitude.

Bob Books® Collections:

Collection 1 — Includes Set 1: Beginning Readers and part of Set 2: Advancing Beginners

Collection 2 — Includes part of Set 2: Advancing Beginners and Set 3: Word Families

Collection 3 — Includes Set 4: Complex Words and Set 5: Long Vowels

Ask for Bob Books at your local bookstore, or visit www.bobbooks.com.

ISBN 0-545-02712-8

6 5 4 3 2   10 11/0

Printed in China   68
This edition first printing, September 2007

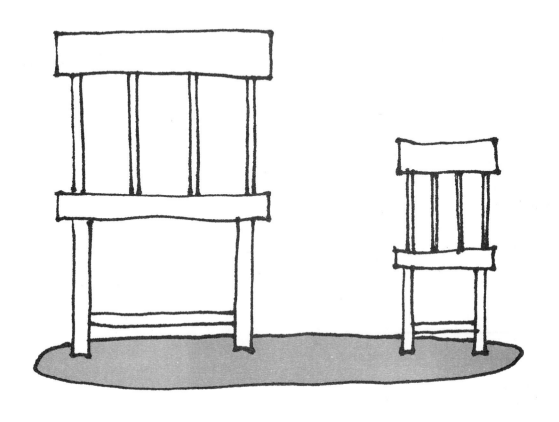

Chicken Big and Chicken Little had two chairs, a big chair and a little chair.

"Who will get the big chair?"
said Chicken Little.

"Who will get
the little chair?" said Chicken Big.

"Let us play a game," they said.
"One, two, three , GO!"

Chicken Big chased Chicken Little across the room.

Chicken Little sat in the big chair.

Chicken Big cheered and clapped her wings.

Chicken Little got up. She chased Chicken Big.

Chicken Big sat in the
little chair.

Chicken Little cheered and clapped her wings.

But all of a sudden, the little
chair creaked, croaked, and BROKE!

Chicken Big crashed to the ground.

Chicken Little ran to her friend.
"O.K., Chicken Big?" she said.

Chicken Big checked her wings.
She checked her legs.
She nodded her head.

"O.K., Chicken Little", she bravely said.

"Then let's play another game,"
said Chicken Little.

"One, two, three, GO!" and off they ran.

Chicken Little ran to the big chair.

Chicken Big ran to the big chair.

They sat down together, and
as far as I know, they are
sitting there still.

The End

Book 15 contains:

Blend:
ch   -   chicken

Vowel Combinations:
ie   -   friend
ea   -   head